George Henry Borrow, Frederick Cerny

Logroño

A Metric Drama

George Henry Borrow, Frederick Cerny

Logroño
A Metric Drama

ISBN/EAN: 9783337333966

Printed in Europe, USA, Canada, Australia, Japan

Cover: Foto ©Andreas Hilbeck / pixelio.de

More available books at **www.hansebooks.com**

LOGROÑO

A Metric Drama in Two Acts

BY

FREDERICK CERNY

WITH TWENTY-NINE ILLUSTRATIONS

BY T. WALTER WILSON

London:

MARCUS WARD & CO., 67 & 68, CHANDOS STREET

AND ROYAL ULSTER WORKS, BELFAST

1877

LOGROÑO.

A METRIC DRAMA IN TWO ACTS.

ALVAREZ in ACT I. a Student of Logroño.

     ,,   in ACT II. an Alchemist.

REA in ACT I. Daughter of the Queen of the Gypsies

    ,,   in ACT II. Queen of the Gypsies.

PEPITA in ACT I. Queen of the Gypsies.

PEDRO in ACT II. a former friend of ALVAREZ.

SALAZAR in ACT II. Son of ALVAREZ and REA.

THE COUNT OF LOGROÑO.

THE ALCALDE OF LOGROÑO.

COURTIERS.

BURGHERS.

A FRIAR.

A CHARLATAN.

PEASANTS, FLOWER GIRLS, ETC.

Twenty years elapse between the First and Second Acts.

NOTE.

—•••—

FOR the story on which the following Drama is based,
you are asked to look to the *Gypsies of Spain*, by George
Borrow (Third Edition, chap. iii., called the " Bookseller
of Logroño ").

FREDERICK CERNY.

LOGROÑO.

ACT I.

SCENE I.

The Market-place of Logroño, a little before sunset. A Fair.
PRIESTS, PEASANTS, CONJURORS, &c. MARKET GIRLS *selling*
flowers. REA *and* PEPITA. *The* COUNT *and* COURTIERS.

Choruses of MARKET GIRLS.

Chorus I.

Fair flowers! sweet flowers!

Fresh flowers, kind lady,

To plant in your bowers,

So fragrant and shady.

B

Violets of blushing blue,
　Fresh from the brake ;
Lilies of waxen hue
　From the still lake.

Chorus II.

Housewife and matron,
　See ! here for you
Are blossoms of citron,
　With myrtle and rue.'

Here is the laurel,
　The sage, and the lime,
The olive and sorrel,
　The sweet-scented thyme

CHARLATAN.

Behold ! the magic topaz ring,
Which doth fame and honour bring.
Wear this ring upon your hand,
Earth shall be at your command.
You who would be great and high,
Seize the happy chance and buy !

FRIAR.

Vanity ! vanity ! there is no fame
In odour can vie with a pious man's name.

CHARLATAN.

Here's the stone may now be bought
Which sages have long ages sought :

Of which one single rub's enough
To turn to gold the basest stuff.
Lo! this piece of worthless lead
Is changed to gold of purest red.
Would you roll in luxury,
Seize the happy chance and buy!

FRIAR.

Vanity! vanity! riches are naught,
Unless to the care of the Church they are brought.

CHARLATAN.

What is honour? what is gold
To this liquid which I hold,
Of potent virtues manifold?
Wrought in most propitious hour,
When the waning moon has power,
From the rare Arabian flower.
A single drop upon the tongue
Makes the oldest grey-beard young.
You, then, who would never die,
Seize the happy chance and buy!

FRIAR.

Vanity! vanity! life is a load,
Unless good Saint Peter has shown you the road.

CHARLATAN.

Here's the famed Egyptian glass,
In which he who buys may view

All things which shall come to pass,
  Mirror'd faithfully and true.
Absent faces may be seen,
Things which are and which have been.
Here a maid may clearly see
Who her future lord shall be.
Here old age may learn the day

When his breath shall pass away.
Any place in any clime
Here is seen. Seize, then, the time,
Ere the chance for ever pass.
Buy! buy! buy my magic glass.

FRIAR.

  Vanity! vanity! Children, give heed!

From me you may purchase rich treasures indeed :
  Stones which the blessed Saint Stephanus slew ;
Tears of the Virgin, which quickly can cure
Each ill of the spirit or bodily sore ;
Here 's a nail from the Ark ; the last chip of the
    cross ;
  Leaves of a palm that in Golgotha grew ;
From Anthony's cavern here 's ever-fresh moss ;
Pardons for all the misdeeds you have done,
  As well as for those which you ever can do ;
  Nails of the saints, strung together as beads ;
Teeth of the Fathers who martyrdom won ;
  An image which every high holiday bleeds.

                          [*The Peasants buy.*]

Go forth abroad ! the Holy Land redeem,
  Which heathen nations trample on in scorn !
Wrest from the infidel the sacred beam,
  The knotted scourge and the sharp crown of
    thorn.
Ye princes, sell your castles and your lands ;
  Merchants, your argosies upon the flood.
Rescue the types of peace from heathen hands,
  And wash them clean in unbeliever's blood.
Leave palace, cottage ; leave ye sire and wife !
Gird up your loins for this heaven-favour'd strife !

CHARLATAN.
  H'st ! hist ! a word apart !

FRIAR.

This way, my son; with all my heart!

CHARLATAN.

Most reverend Father, in your store
You have the Virgin's tears to cure
All kinds of maladies, I think?

FRIAR.

'Tis this, my son; you've but to drink
Some thirty drops, and straight you'll feel
A glow of health from heel to heel.

CHARLATAN.

Here, then, is gold!

FRIAR.   Gold so well spent
Is gold not lost, but only lent.
But give me of your crystal clear,
Wherein all future things appear!

CHARLATAN.

Behold!

FRIAR.   Here's gold!

CHARLATAN.   And gold gets gold,
As heat gets heat and cold gets cold.
                    [*They separate.*]

Chorus of MARKET GIRLS.

Chorus I. *and* II.

Buy our sweet roses,
  Breathing perfume!
Buy our pale lilies,
  Fragrant in bloom!

For sages the roots are,
  Of magical powers;
For housewives the fruits are,
  For lovers the flowers.

How poor is the palace
  Where flowers are not!
But, graced by their chalice,
  How rich is the cot!

Pluck'd in the morning,
  The dew on them hung
As bright as the dawning
  Of love on the young.

Hid from day's glances,
  Away in the shade,
Like half-conscious fancies
  Of some bashful maid,

They closed to the noonbeams
  Each treasure of bliss,
To open to moonbeam's
  Sweet passionate kiss.

Cherish, protect them,
  Their smile shall repay;
Scorn them, reject them,
  They wither away.

REA.

My mother! let us leave this noisy scene:
  My heart is faint.
Why did we quit the silence of the woods,
  And the sweet scent
Of the gem-sprinkled meadows? Let us go!

PEPITA.

Stay, daughter, yet awhile!
To-day I must win gold.

REA.

Nay, I beseech thee, mother, come away!
  There is a man,

Gaudily dressed, who follows all our steps.
    Where'er I turn,
His eyes are on me with a hateful glance :
    And at his side
Companions laugh, and point, and urge him on.

PEPITA.

Ah ! let me see the fool.
Why, daughter, 'tis the Count !
The sickly pale-faced cur.
Dare he to lift his eyes
In rudeness on my child ?
They say his will is law.
'Tis well for Spanish dogs.
But, daughter, thou art right :
Let us depart in haste !

COUNT.

Now, by my faith, as I 'm a gentleman,
You is the brightest wench we 've seen to-day.
Look at her carriage ! it is like a queen's ;
Nay, queens we wot of are not half as straight ;
While on her head, for regal diadem,
Are wound the rich dark masses of her hair.

1st COURTIER.

Ah ! well enough ! yes, doubtless, well enough !
But, for my taste, a shade too swarthy too.

C

COUNT.

> Yourself are half a Moor. Of course your rage
> Is all for blonde-haired beauties, golden Goths.
> Would she but lift her eyes, methink their fire
> Would light her darkness as the stars the night.

2nd COURTIER.

> She seems to know that you regard her, Count,
> And keeps her eyes on the less ardent earth.

COUNT.

> Yes, well I know their pretty bashful ways,
> These artful witches ! and the wiles and lures
> With which they chain us while they feign to shun.
> It were a crying scandal and a shame
> To let her pine and wait and watch alone.
> Let me go smell this darkly blushing rose.

3rd COURTIER.

> Pardon, my lord ! I would not spoil your sport ;
> But this young witch is half a witch indeed.
> Nay, more, if what I hear be soothly said,
> That strange old wizened creature at her side
> Is the true queen of witches ; and the child
> Is her sole daughter.

COUNT.   I take thee not ; be plain !

3rd COURTIER.

> There is a tribe of vagrants lately come

Into these parts; but whence or why they came
No one can tell. Some say from Egypt's plains;
Some, from Bohemia. Some do even affirm
That they are of the tribes of Israel lost.
This much is certain, that their private speech
Is an outlandish jargon of their own.
But stranger still their lives! In woods and glens
They lurk, and live like Arabs under tents.
The men are jockeys, blacksmiths, tinkers, thieves;
The women witches, fortune-tellers, thieves.

COUNT.

"Tis strange! I'll speak with them.
Await me here. I see they move away.

[*Crosses over.*]

COUNT.

Good evening, mother!

PEPITA.   Give thee good evening, Count.

COUNT.

I see you know my rank.

PEPITA.   'Mongst other things

COUNT.

As what?

PEPITA.   Your nature.

COUNT.

Ha! that is well; my nature's good, they say.

PEPITA.

As is an owl's, that drones away the day.
But ask the little birds if he be good,
Whom he despoils in farmyard and in wood.

COUNT *to* REA.

Believe it not! I'm not so bad, fair maid;
My claws are velvet when I'm not gainsaid.
Then, if you like, I can be harsh indeed.

PEPITA.

Threaten the cowards who your threatenings heed.

COUNT.

Methinks that few can boast they do not fear
My anger.

PEPITA.   True! but two of them are here.

COUNT.

Enough! What do ye in the fair to-day?

PEPITA.

Tell fools their fortunes; that is, fools who pay.

COUNT.

I'll take thy "fool" if thou wilt take my gold.
Now thou art paid, my fortune must be told.

PEPITA.

Lend me thy hand! Seest thou this line of life
So deep and smooth? That tells of little strife
And much of pleasure. Ha! take back thy hand,
Take back thy gold!

COUNT.   Continue, I command!

PEPITA.

Take back thy gold, I say! I dare not read
Thy fortune further.

COUNT.   I bid thee still proceed!

PEPITA.

A bloody death cuts short thy middle course;
No time is there for sorrow or remorse.

COUNT.

Peace, wretched hag! else shalt thou straight be
bound
And stoned for sorcery, or burnt, or drown'd.

PEPITA.

The raven scorns the owl. My daughter, come!
To please a fool one must be knave or dumb.

COUNT.

Thou hast a nimble tongue. 'Tis well for thee
Thou hast a lovely child, if thine she be;
I'll take the payment for thy saucy speech
From her sweet lips, a separate fine from each.

PEPITA.

Stand back, I warn thee; or the doom I read
I shall myself fulfil and strike thee dead.
See how he quakes! this hero with his brag,
At an old woman's arm, "a wretched hag."
My daughter, come! nor fear the man who fears
Both present death and fate of future years.

[REA *and* PEPITA *hurry off.*]

[COUNT *crosses back to his companions.*]

1st COURTIER.

> Well, Count! methinks thy suing went amiss;
> Thy Queen seem'd loath to have thy homaged kiss
> And the Queen Mother, if I judged aright
> Look'd on thy wooing in no pleasant light.

COUNT.

> Now, by my countly word, I'll let her know
> She dare not treat a Spanish noble so.
> Come ye with me, pursue this arrant witch;
> Burnt shall she be, and buried in a ditch,
> Her daughter be my mistress for a day;
> Then he who lists may have her. Come away!

SCENE II.

An open forest-glade a few miles from Logroño. Early night.
Moonlight. ALVAREZ and PEASANTS. The older PEASANTS
are seated round the younger, who dance and sing.

PEASANTS *dance and sing.*

Sound the shrill pipe and the cheery-voiced horn!
    Castanets rattle! and strike the loud tabor!
Wake the red blush of the dew-laden morn!
    They only know leisure who earn it with labour.

            Swift o'er the mead
                Our nimble feet glancing,
            The night-hours shall speed
                With music and dancing.

Stars, high above,
  Our own hearts resemble ;
In joy and in love
  They glow and they tremble.

Round on the sod,
  Old folks on the daisies
Murmur and nod
  And whisper our praises.

Feeble are they,
  And dimm'd are their glances ;
They think of the day
  They led the swift dances.

Silent in dreams
  All nature rejoices,
Bathed in moonbeams
  And lull'd by our voices.

Cloudlet with shade
  The meadow may cover;
There's light in the glade
  Enough for the lover.

Bright though the skies
  Hang glittering o'er us,
Brighter the eyes
  That are dancing before us.
Rise, echo, arise !
  And join in the chorus.

Sound the shrill pipe and the cheery-voiced horn !
  Castanets rattle ! and strike the loud tabor !
Wake the red blush of the dew-laden morn !
  They only know leisure who earn it with labour.

Enter REA *and* PEPITA *hurriedly.*

REA.

  I can no further, mother : I am faint.
  Let us, I pray thee, rest awhile amidst
  This village festival.   Mothers are here
  And happy maidens.   There are fathers here
  Who will not see two hapless women wrong'd.
  It is so far unto our tented home.
  And much I dread the men who dog our steps,
  But wait a lonelier road to do us harm.

PEPITA.

  If these were gypsies we were safe indeed.
  But trust them not ; it is a coward race.
  Yet, since no refuge offers in our strait,
  Do thou bide here and mingle with the dance,
  While I—a murrain on these feeble limbs !—
  Press onward to our people in the camp
  And summon help to whip the curs away.   [*Goes.*]

REA. [*Aside.*]

  How strangely sound these tones of revelry,
  These murmuring notes of peaceful happiness,

Unto a bosom full of anxious thoughts.
I feel as must the over-hunted deer,
Which seeks a refuge from the cruel chase
Amidst the farmyard denizens. Alas!
Perchance as groundless is my hope to hide

As is the hart's among the low-neck'd kine;
Perchance are these as impotent to shield
From threaten'd ill, as are the timorous sheep
To dare the dogs that bay the panting deer.

[*Draws her dagger from her bosom and replaces it.*]

One friend have I which the poor brute has not,
A friend who will not fail me at my need.

ALVAREZ. [*Approaches.*]
Pardon me, maiden, if I'm overbold!
Nor deem it rudeness that I thus intrude
Upon your presence. But you seem alone,

And, as I judge from dress and other signs,
A stranger to these parts.   Is there, then, aught—
Trust me, I ask it in all courtesy—
Wherein I can but serve you ?   Do not pause,
But be assured it were a generous act
To bid me be the servant of your will.

REA.

I thank you truly for your kindness, sir;
But Heaven forbid that I should want your aid.

ALVAREZ.

Nay ! that's unkind, an undeserv'd rebuke.
Believe me, too, that I had said the same
Even to the oldest ugliest woman here,
If I had thought that my poor services
Might be required, even as I spoke to you
Who 'tis no flattery to say are fair.

REA.

Forgive me, gentle sir,
That, in my trouble, I weigh'd not my words.
I would have said, the only help I lack
May be of such a kind that I would fain
It were not render'd, even for both our sakes.

ALVAREZ.

Speak it, I pray you, and my arm is yours;

For I am sure as that a heaven's above
'Tis naught that misbeseems a gentleman.

REA.

Briefly, then, thus.   My mother and myself
Were in Logroño's market-place to-day,
Where we were used with insult and abuse;
And, as we left and hurried on our way,
We were pursued.   So, by the greatest haste,
By turning through the woodland's devious ways,
Known to my mother better than to them
Who dogg'd our footsteps, are we hither come.
My mother left me to seek aid at home:
My only hope is here to hide unfound.

ALVAREZ.

It was a shameful and a dastard act!
Learnt you the name of him who used you so?

REA.

His name I heard not: he was called the Count.

ALVAREZ.

Ha!

REA.

Why do you start and darkly knit your brows?

ALVAREZ.

'Tis nothing, nothing!

[*Aside.*] A serious matter too;
For well, I wot, these cow'd and armless hinds
Will scarcely stand the brunt of flashing steel.

REA.

What do you murmur?   Is there hope for me?
Will not these peasants lift their hands to save
A poor defenceless girl from cruel wrong?

ALVAREZ.

Hope is there ever; and one arm at least,
If need be, will not fail thee.   But meanwhile
Rest on the sward behind this spreading tree
Seeking concealment.   By this fitful light
The peasants will not see but thou art one
Of their own number resting from the dance.

REA. [*Giving her hand.*]

How shall I thank you for your courtesy?
To-day I thought all Spaniards were alike,
And that I needs must hate you all alike;
But now—— [*Pauses.*]

ALVAREZ.   Continue, maiden, pray!

REA.

But now, but now—would that my mother came!

[*Music.*]

PEASANTS *dance and sing.*

Home from the river and home from the lea
  The sweet breathing kine are come drowsily lowing;
But this is the hour that for you, love, and me
  Sets the heart merrily dancing and glowing.

        Above, as we turn,
          And wheel in our dancing.
        The fire-flies burn,
          So merrily glancing.

      We dance to the sound
        Of scraping and drumming;
      They wheel in their round
        To chafers' low humming.

      The cloud dances high
        By the moon brightly beaming,
      The leaf dances by
        From the forest that's dreaming.

      The streamlet, that flows
        With rhythmical motion,
      Sings as it goes
        Far down to the ocean.

Home from the river and home from the lea
  The sweet breathing kine are come drowsily lowing;
But this is the hour that for you, love, and me
  Sets the heart merrily dancing and glowing.

Enter the COUNT *and* COURTIERS.

COUNT.

 Peace, noisy hounds!   Is this your loyalty?

   [*Music stops.*   PEASANTS *rise, uncover,*
       and huddle together.]

 Is this the lesson I have taught ye, boors?
 Does it beseem your base and brutal souls
 To dance and sing when your liege lord is here?

1*st* PEASANT.

 Pardon, my lord!   we knew not you were nigh.

COUNT.

 Peace, dotard!   But bring forth
 The wretched harridan and her pretty child
 Who hide among you now.   I say, bring forth!

1*st* PEASANT.

 My Lord!   we know of none such; we are all
 Your Lordship's humble and devoted serfs.

COUNT.

 Old man, you lie.   They could not have escaped.

2*nd* PEASANT.

 I think I saw two strangers while ago;
 But now I see them not; they must be gone.

Count.

If you do find them not—— Stay! who are you,
Old greybeard?

3rd Peasant.   Ninety years and odd.

Count.

What! dare you mock me, man?

1st Peasant Girl.

Pardon him, gracious Lord; my grandsire's deaf
And nearly blind. He knows you not, my lord!
Nor what he says. Have pity, noble Lord!

Count.

Bring the old idiot hither.
                    [*Draws his dagger and holds it near
                              3rd* Peasant's *face.*]
Seest thou this blade?

3rd Peasant.

Why aye! aye! aye! 'Twas I that made the blade,
As good a blade as e'er Toledo wrought.
'Twas done for you just sixty years ago,
Come Whitsuntide—ah, no! your grandsire though,
When he went fighting with the swarthy Moors.
A noble count, ah me! merry withal!
I mind the day as yesterday he came
Into my shop. He always had a jest
    E

And pleasant word for poor men like myself:
Said he——

COUNT.   Out, cursed driveller. [*Strikes him.*]
Seize this old fool and bind him to yon tree.

[1*st and* 2*nd* COURTIERS *bind* 3*rd* PEASANT.]

Now tell me, you who value this old life,
Where are the gypsies whom you hide away?
For drop by drop his watery blood shall fall
Until I find them.

1*st* PEASANT GIRL, *kneeling.*
    I do beseech thee, harm him not, my Lord!
    Say 'tis a jest; but push it not too far,
    Lest the last spark of his vitality,
    With very fright, do leave his feeble frame.

COUNT. [*Spurns her.*]

    A forfeit! take this puling wench away,

                        [*To 1st* COURTIER.]

    And, for your trouble, she shall be your booty.

    Now, once more! Are you dumb?

    Stand round me, friends, and with our dagger-points

    We'll soon unloose his obstinate old tongue.

                [*Pricks him with his dagger.*

          REA *advances from behind the tree.*

COUNT.

    Ha! ha! one bird at least is caught.

              [REA *cuts the cords with her knife.*

REA.

    It shall not be.

    What! are ye men, or stones,

    To stand unmoved and see this old man's blood?

    O! would to heaven

    That I were not a weak

    And helpless woman, or that a man were here!

    Out, paltry hinds!

    Richly ye merit all

    The wrong and tyranny that falls on ye;

    For slaves are made

    For stripes and bitter words,

    Nor ill can happen more than their desert.

Count.

> Prettily mouth'd, in sooth !
> Thy teaching is so sound
> That I should like to hear
> Thy lessons many times.

> > [Rea *retires up the stage.*]

> Seize her ! and bring her back.

> > [*2nd* Courtier *seizes* Rea.]

[*To* Peasants.]

> For you, you may begone.
> But let this teach you, curs,
> Never to thwart my will,
> That I am like a lion
> Who must be lord of all.

> > [Peasants *go.*]

Rea.

> Base-blooded race !

> > [*Shakes off 2nd* Courtier.]

> I know not if you earn
> My scorn or pity most.

[*To* Count.]

> But you, more cowardly still !
> For that you trade upon
> The fears of other men.
> But I defy your power.

Learn that a gypsy's hand
Can set a gypsy free.
Farewell, my mother dear !
Fair earth, dear life, farewell !

> [REA *will stab herself* ; ALVAREZ *springs forward,*
> *seizes her dagger.*]

ALVAREZ.

Another sheath for thy knife
Than thy innocent breast shall be found.

> [*Draws his sword.*]

[*To* COUNT *and* COURTIERS.]
Out, coward vulture brood !
Or stand and draw like men.
What ! are four nobles here
And not one gentleman ?
Nay, then you have no need
To wear these useless tools.

> [*Takes sword from the* COUNT, *strikes him and*
> *drives him and* COURTIERS *off. A pause·*
> REA *takes* ALVAREZ'S *hand.*]

REA.

Brave, noble friend ! my niggard tongue is mute
To the rich wishes of my grateful heart.
How poor is a poor maiden !   Only thanks
(Though warmest, deepest) for a noble deed !

ALVAREZ.

    Fain would I bid thee cease,

    Nor shame with thanks the smallness of my deed,

    But that 'tis very sweet

    To hear the music of thy voice, and see

    The glow upon thy cheek

    As the bright glances sparkle in thine eyes.

REA.

    And I would thank thee still

    And yet again. For I do love to dwell

    Upon thy generous act;

For thus it seems sweet gratitude doth grow,
And growing find excuse
For its excess which so usurps my heart.

ALVAREZ.

Speak it again, sweet maid!
Say 'twas a noble, most chivalrous deed;
Say that thy heart is stirred
To its most secret nook—that ne'er before
Was it so deeply moved:
And I will drink thy words, nor blush to hear.

REA.

All this I say and more.
I feel that I could almost hate a man
Who did me equal deed;
For then my gratitude would, being split,
Be, like a broken gem,
Not half as precious as it was entire.

ALVAREZ.

And I, too; I would hate
The man who won thy gratitude—and still
Would hate him even more
Did he not serve thee in thy need as I.
It is most wrong; but yet
The sweeetness of it doth o'ermask the wrong.

REA.

> I hear the far sound
> Of my people who come to my rescue.
> > Hasten away !
> They are hasty and quick in their anger,
> And may not endure
> The face of a stranger at present.

ALVAREZ.

> Straight to Logroño I must hie me now,
> And there await a challenge from the Count ;
> For if he have a spark of manhood left,
> His sword and mine must cross, and one must fall ;
> But if he dare not meet me, I 'll proclaim
> Him dastard in the face of all his court.

REA.

> Nay, I beseech you, trust him not, my love ;
> He would not scruple to betray your faith,
> Nor stand on honour if he gained his end.

ALVAREZ.

> Yet must I stand on honour. When I smote
> He had no sword ; and therefore am I bound.

REA.

> If you return not ere three days are spent,
> I, woman as I am, must seek you out.

ALVAREZ.

No, I command! what ill may light on me
Must not be shared by you.   Remain away,
Or send one of your tribe to search for me.

REA.

Now go! now go!

ALVAREZ.

I go, but leave with thee
Half of my being; pray thee, guard it well!

REA.

I 'll hide it in my heart
And tend it with most jealous watchfulness.

ALVAREZ.

Hast thou no gift for me,
Which I may cherish in my banishment?

REA.

Not one but this,   [*They kiss.*]
Such as I give my mother when we part.

[ALVAREZ *goes.*]

F

SCENE III.

(DUMB SHOW.)

Early dawn.

Banquet-hall in COUNT LOGROÑO'S *Palace.*

One torch nearly burnt out.

Disorder after a revel.

The COUNT *and* GUESTS *are reclining in various attitudes, asleep.*

Enter, behind, REA.

She advances to the table, sees the keys of the dungeon under the COUNT'S *hand.*

Stands uncertain.

Advances and touches the keys.

The COUNT *stirs and* REA *retires.*

Rea snatches up a knife.
The torch goes out.
The Count is heard to fall and groan.
Pause.
Rattle of keys.

The door at back opens, and REA *stands upon the threshold.*

Her form is seen against the light of the early dawn.

Distant chorus of PEASANTS *coming to Market.*

Chorus of PEASANTS.

Awake! the hue of morning
    Is creeping o'er the skies;
The morrow's light is dawning,
    Awake! awake! arise!
            Arise!

Awake! the nimble swallow
    In wheeling circuit flies!

The owl's voice in the hollow
Sounds fainter still and dies.
Arise !

The hawk has plumed his feather ;
The fawn stirs in the brake ;
There 's a blush upon the heather,
And a smile upon the lake.
Arise !

There 's light upon the river ;
There 's light upon the mead,
Where trembling dewdrops quiver
Around the daisy's head.
Arise !

Though shadows still are clinging
Down where the forest lies,
Yet even there are singing
The merry birds.   Arise !
Arise !

SCENE IV.

Early morning.   A Dungeon in the Palace of COUNT
LOGROÑO.   ALVAREZ *fettered.*

ALVAREZ.

Sweet vision, stay! O fade not yet! not yet!
Fair dream, why art thou vanished?   Fall again
Upon my hungering senses!   Ah me! ah me!
Better not sleep, to see bright sunny fields,
Green trees, and whispering rivers, soaring birds,
Than, dreaming so, to wake and see these bars,
Mocking with phantom-like reality.
O! sweet oblivion! why dost thou disdain
To smooth a captive's pillow?   Rest, downy rest,

Which blesses labour's couch, is fled from mine;
For mine is but the weary spirit's toil,
Which earneth no repose—with dreams so bright
That they should wholly cease or else endure
For evermore unfading and unchanged.
Freedom! the freeman never knows thy worth;
For thou art like a gentle mother's love,
Not rightly honour'd until wholly lost.
The chillness creeping through my prison-bars,
Warns me that night doth wane. Night! what is
    night
To one whose days are darkness? Time, friend of
    man,
Thou art the captive's bitterest enemy:
Thy leaden feet, unhurried by his prayers,
Drag slowly on, mocking his bursting heart—
Most tardy in his greatest misery.

    Chorus of Peasants *going to market.*

      Awake! the hue of morning
        Is creeping o'er the skies;
           &c., &c.

Alvarez.

Once more the morning rests upon the hills,
And summons all things on the earth to life.
All things but me—me to the night of death,
Or to the life of light which knows no darkening,

And to the light of life which knows no dying.
The hour has come, that one pre-eminent hour,
When the long yearning soul at length shall know
The truth or baselessness of things foretold—
If that our dreams be tricks of fantasy,
Wrought in our being by the unseen hand
For some beneficent end not understood,
Or that they form the one reality,
While earthly life is but a nightmare trance,
Untrue, unhappy, and unprofitable.
Still is the earth, as one sweet garden, fair;
While the dread bridge by which we pass from life
Sways awful o'er the gulf Uncertainty,
Whose opposite shore is wrapt in mists and night.
Who feels no tremor as he treads that bridge
Is more or less than man—a god or fool.

       [The door is unlocked.]

The door is moved—the door which leads
From deadly life to living death.
Ha! what are these?

      [Enter REA.]

Can they be things of life
Who glide as noiseless as the sailing clouds?
I know them both,
Yet know them not like this—
So strange, so weird, and so unnatural.
Speak! be ye flesh?

Or be ye but a dream

Summon'd by supreme suffering from my soul

Begone! begone!

And let my last short hour

Be given to hopes of heaven, not shades of hell.

REA.

    H'sh!   Know'st thou me not?

ALVAREZ.

    Thou art indeed

    Of flesh and not a ghost.

    But wherefore dost thou visit me like this?

    By what strange power

    G

Hast thou unloosed the bolts
And gain'd access where not even daylight comes?
And, see! thy feet
Are dabbled o'er with blood.
What does the Count behind thee, with one hand
Press'd on his breast,
Whence issues blood apace?
But O! most horrible! it staineth not the stones.

REA.

The Count?

ALVAREZ.

The other hand
Still points to thee and me,
Then turns its finger to its gaping wound.

REA.

I see it not! 'Tis but
Thy suffering fantasy.
Come, hasten! quit this place!
The guards are bribed, or lie
Drunken and full of sleep.

ALVAREZ.

Even as I gaze
The shade has passed away;
So comes my heart into my breast again.

But, maiden, say
What dost thou here to-night?
Daring the dangers of this house of crime?
Art thou, as I,
A victim of his rage?
Have, then, his toils at last encompass'd thee?
Most bitter thought!
For if thou art not free,
My life were sacrificed for naught indeed.

REA.

Trouble thyself no more.
No more the Count shall lift
His hand against thy peace;
For in his blood he lies
A bleeding, stiffening corpse.

ALVAREZ.

And thy white hand
Is red with his vile blood!
And thou hast struck this wretched man to death!

REA.

I have.

ALVAREZ.

Out! shame, O shame!
Did I not see thee once

Turn thy sharp knife against thine own pure breast?
But now thy blade
Has sent a shuddering soul
Unshriven to judgment with a load of crimes.

REA.

You blow was for myself;
But this was struck for thee.
O bid me not feel shame
That, for thy sake, I smote;
For if my arm had fail'd
Never wouldst thou have seen
The shadows slanting east.
Didst thou not strike for me,
Saving from worse than death?
Though wild the gypsies' blood,
Their hearts know gratitude.

ALVAREZ.

My child! my child!
By this red deed hast thou
Placed thy young soul in cruel jeopardy.

REA.

O! chide me not! my people's laws
. Are built on other code than thine.
O! chide me not! if I did wrong
'Twas for thy sake—ah! for thy sake;
Thy precious life was ransom'd by his death.

ALVAREZ.

Thou principle! thou formula of fools!
I cast thee to the idle winds of earth.
Ye doctrines loudly preach'd, ye laws laid down
To govern crowds, must all be thrown aside
When a supreme occasion shows its front;
Then is the gloss of cities torn away,
While the rough nature of the savage man
Asserts its hidden strong pre-eminence.
So from this hour am I for ever thine;
Thy way shall be my way, thy law my law,
I shall but see the good and ill of life
As they are mirror'd in thy loving soul.

REA.

Joy be mine for ever!
Dearest, let us hasten;
For the sun is climbing
Through the eastern sky.
Quick! the guards will waken.
If we tarry longer
We shall be o'ertaken.
So I loose thy chains.

[*Unlock's* ALVAREZ'S *fetters.*]

ALVAREZ.

Yellowly waves the corn,
Rippling like the sea,

Beneath the blush of morn;
  Come, my love, with me!

Gracefully bend the trees,
  Waving their branches free,
Beneath the waking breeze;
  Come, my love, with me!

REA.

Merrily sings the bird,
  Soaring high o'er the lea,
Faintly its voice is heard;
  Come, my love, with me!

Murmuring flows the stream
  Beneath the willow tree,
Whispering, as in a dream,
  Come, my love, with me!

ALVAREZ.

With thee for ever, sweet, my love,
  To tread the paths of wood and brake,
To watch the glorious stars above,
  To watch the eye of day awake;

With thee to wind the forest ways,
  To feel thy breath upon my cheek,
To dream away the happy days,
  At eve with thee repose to seek;

With thee to seek the waxen flower
   That floats upon the glassy mere,
To find where blushing violets cower,
    And weave them in thy raven hair.

SCENE V.

Same as SCENE II. *Morning.*

Enter ALVAREZ *and* REA.

REA.

      Here we must part, my darling; for, beyond,
      In yonder hollow lies our hidden camp.
      And ere I bring thee to the gypsy tribe
      I must prepare them for thy coming, love.

ALVAREZ.

      Then so, my sweet preserver, fare thee well !
      I haste to hide me in yon tangled wood,
      To count the leaden minutes till thou comest
      Bidding me welcome to thy woodland home;

For henceforth dare I never more return
Back to the haunts of men. My sudden flight,
Coming upon the Count's so bloody end,
Will raise suspicion—nay, great certainty,
That I did slay him as I broke away.

REA.

Say! wilt thou quit thy country and thy home
For my poor sake? Can one young maiden's heart
Replace the thousand luxuries of home?
Ah! it is selfishness that blinds my soul,
And urges me to bid thee cling to me.

ALVAREZ.

Thou art my country, dearest; thou my home.
Where'er thou art my home is at thy feet;
But will thy tribe receive me? I have heard
That they despise a Spaniard as a dog.

REA.

I am, my love, the daughter of their queen.
Brothers have I not one. My sire is dead.
Hence do the wild and uncouth-hearted men
Treat me with deference. My slightest wish
Is law to them. I doubt not they receive
My future husband as their future king.

REA.

  Like the streamlet at our feet
   Our love shall be;

H

Every hinderance it meet
  Shall wake new harmony.
Every rapid, every lake
  Shall be fairer than the last;
Yet so like that it shall wake
  Thought of the past.

ALVAREZ.

Like the evening o'er our heads
  Our love shall be;
Where each glittering planet spreads
  Its rays in majesty.
Every day shall greet our eyes
  With fresh delight,
As every hour new stars arise
  To deck the night.

REA.

Like the bindweed and the sun
  Our love shall be;
When his course of light is run,
  Her soul shall flee.

ALVAREZ.

> When the faithful constant flower
> Hangs her fair head,
> He knows no life beyond that hour—
> His course is sped.

Enter PEPITA *behind.*

ALVAREZ.

> So, from the fountains of thy beauteous eyes,
> Let me drink up the waters of thy soul.
> Through tasting thirst, in thirsting taste again,
> Until my being sinks into the bliss
> Of one long sweet intoxicating draught.

REA.

> Ah, dearest! if mine eyes were seal'd in night,
> Those fountains of my soul dried up, would then
> Thy love be lessen'd?

ALVAREZ.

> Not so, sweet; for then
> I'd catch the fragrance from thy delicate lips,
> As thus and thus, and still my soul should drink
> In sweet delirium of matchless joy.
> Yea! and if thou wouldst still deny thy lips,
> I'd press thee to me thus, and listen so
> To the quick throbbings of thy fluttering heart,
> Which leaps and trembles like a new-caged bird.

REA.

My heart is like a bird
Beating the barriers of its cage, my breast,
To fly and nestle in thy bosom, love.

ALVAREZ.

My bosom is the bush
Where she shall build her little nest of love,
For there my heart shall mate her; they shall dwell
Happy and safe and songful evermore.

[PEPITA *advances.*]

PEPITA.

Accursed be the womb that bore thee!
Accursed be the breasts that fed!
Accursed be the arms that tended!
Thou, my daughter; thou, a quean!
Dallying with the milk-faced stranger!

REA.

Spare me, mother!

PEPITA.

Get thee home!

REA.

Hear me, mother!

PEPITA.

Lips polluted,

Reeking with the recent kisses!
Thou a gypsy! never! never!

ALVAREZ.

For pity's sake deny me not, but listen.

PEPITA.

Babble thy vanities into strumpets' ears
That love the empty folly of thy words.

[*To* REA.]

My daughter! O my daughter!
Thou wert a true pure-hearted daughter once,
Wouldst scorn to meet the stranger in the wood;
So did I rear thee, so did I love thee, child.
But now! to steal away like coward thief,
Hid from my eyes that loved to watch thee so!
To meet a one-day's friend alone. For shame!
While I for six long anxious hours have dragged
From place to place these dull and trembling limbs
Sickened at heart and fearing even to fear.
Wert thou a wanton woman of the town
Thou couldst not act more shamelessly, my child.

ALVAREZ.

Turn thy wrath on me!
But spare thy chidings. If a fault it be
To drink the sweet companionship of love,
Mine be the blame. But crush her not with words

Whom I do love as far beyond myself
As heaven is far beyond the grovelling earth.

PEPITA.

Peace, glib-tongued boy, and go!
I need but whisper to my tribe that thou,
With smooth, soft-spoken words, didst try to turn
The silly fancies of my daughter's brain,
When straight a hundred knives would spring to
    light,
To wipe the stain from her polluted name.
And thou, unhappy child! wouldst be so shunn'd
By all thy playmates of the gypsy race
That not a tent would shield thee from the storm,
No hand be stretch'd to help thy utmost need;
But thou wouldst be deserted, till thy life
Dragg'd to its end of misery and want.
Come, then, my daughter!

ALVAREZ.

Now heaven forgive the blindness of thy rage!
For that thou art the mother of my love,
And that upon thy bosom, now so toss'd
In heedless passion, once my love did rest,
And kiss'd thy cruel lips, I pardon thee!
I pity thee! But O! for pity's sake,
Confound not love as true and pure as ours
With the false dalliance of an idle hour.

Our love must last as long as lasts our life.
Yea! and in death shall gather wings of life
To bear it to the bourn beyond the sky.

PEPITA.

So talk they all, my daughter. Come away!
And swear that never once from this hour forth
Wilt thou hold converse, or by word or look,
With this false-hearted fool.
Swear it that he may hear!
By thy mother's fame,
By thy father's name,
By the land of the rising sun.

ALVAREZ.

Forbear! forbear! O! call not, I implore,
As witness of this most unnatural oath,
Aught that is sacred. Woman, do not dare
To mell the things which lie beyond thy scope
With earthly passions.

PEPITA.

Swear!

[REA *kneels before* PEPITA.]

REA.

Spurn me not from thy feet, mother!
As thus before thee I kneel:

I never thwarted thy wishes, mother,
　　But loved thee with all my heart.
Spare me, spare me this oath, mother!
　　I dare not swear as you bid.

How can I swear to forsake him
　　Who is dearer to me than myself?
Ask me to pluck from their sockets
　　These eyes that are blinded by tears;

But, O! ask me not, I beseech thee,
To yield up the love of my soul!

PEPITA.

Between, then, the love of thy mother
And that of this boy hast thou chosen.
The love of a score of slow seasons
For that of one hour hast thou barter'd.
Did I not bear thee in anguish,
Tend thee in want and in sickness,
Shield thee from blasts of the tempest,
The pitiless rays of the noonday,
Tear from my shivering bosom
The last tatter'd fragment to wrap thee
When the snow and the sleet pelted on us!
Yea! as thou grewest in beauty,
From evils more dreaded I shielded.
Far from the eyes of the wanton,
Remote in the dell and the forest,
Thou grewest in purity ever.
And love such as this dost thou trample,
Devotion like this dost thou scorn,
For madness of one foolish moment.
Swear! swear! or I curse thee and go

REA.

O deem not that I love thee less
Because I love him so;

I

Nor think that I can e'er forget
  My gratitude to thee.
The rolling year, that bringeth change
  To all upon the earth,
Shall only bring my love increase
  For thee and for our tribe.
Tell me, my mother, I implore,
  Why chidest thou this love?

PEPITA.

  Because along his veins
  The pale blood of our foes
  Oozes its sluggish way;
  Because there is no word
  As strong as is the scorn
  Which every gypsy feels
  For his accursed race;
  Because not even once,
  Since first we saw this land,
  Has gypsy blood been stain'd
  By mingling with this mud;
  Because I'd rather see
  Thee rotting at my feet
  Than looking without hate
  Upon the paltry crew.
  Enough, my child! now swear
  Never again to look
  Upon this coward boy.

REA.

> Ha! mother, say not so!
> For it is false, although my mother speaks,
> I say 'tis false! 'tis false!
> Though all the rest were cowards in their
> hearts,
> My love at least is brave,
> Who rescued me from insult and from shame
> One against many foes.

PEPITA.

> A plot to trap a silly maiden's heart.
> When I was young I was as fair as thou;
> But thrice when wanton hands were laid on
> me,
> Thrice has this dagger drunk the Spaniard's
> blood.
> Where was thy dagger, child?

ALVAREZ.

> Her heart was as firm as thine own,
> Her dagger was pluck'd from its sheath;
> But the point was not turn'd to her foes,
> It was turn'd to her own virgin breast.
> Had not my arm stayed the blow,
> And, wringing the blade from her hand,
> Driven the dogs from their prey,
> Thy daughter had fall'n in her blood.

PEPITA.

> And better so! for so may gypsies die.
> My only child! my age's only prop,
> Far better so. That keen and searching steel
> Had cleft a passage for thy maiden soul.
> Cruel preserver! thou a deadlier blow
> Hast dealt, a blow more pitiable—
> Hast planted in the bosom thou hast saved
> A festering cancer, hatefuller than death.
> But quick, my child: the oath! the oath! the
>   oath!

REA.

> Mother, I cannot!

PEPITA.

> 'Tis well!
> A mother's love poised 'gainst a lover's lips
> Has kick'd the beam. 'Tis well. 'Tis very
>   well.
> A mother's order and a people's will
> Weigh as two feathers in thine idiot scale.
> 'Tis well, again! But one more weight I'll
>   cast,
> My hate unceasing and unquenchable.
> Swear! or I blight thee with a gypsy's curse.

REA.

> Mother, have mercy on thine only child!

PEPITA.

> I had a daughter once : she is no more.
> A mother's curse shall rest upon thy head
> If thou refusest. All thy ways be clogg'd,
> Even when my scanty breath is spent at last,
> With the undying hatred of the dead.

ALVAREZ.

> Swear not ! for love
> Is stronger than hate.
> Hatred shall pass
> Like a cloud from the sky,
> Like breath from a glass.
> Enduring as Fate,
> As the planets above,
> Love lives for aye.

REA.

> I cannot, dare not swear.
> O ! my poor heart, that ever I was born
> To meet thy frown, who ever smiled on me,
> To disobey thee ? Yet it must be so.

PEPITA.

> Come lightnings and blast thee for ever !
> Diseases consume thee unceasing !
> May every heart which thou lovest
>   Wither and dwindle apace !

Thy beauty be turned to corruption!
Thy strength to the racking of agues!
Thy children be curses about thee!
  Thy friends be as false as thyself!
The love, for which now thou rebellest,
Be turned to a jest and a hissing!
Thy mornings bring sorrow and wailing.
  Dark be thy nights with despair.
Then, when thou desolate liest,
Heart-broken, forsaken, and dying,
Think of thy mother, who. cursed thee—
  Think of thy mother, and die!

REA.

  Mercy! mercy! [*Faints.*]

PEPITA.

  Thy sex shall upbraid thee!
  Thy tribe shall forsake thee!

ALVAREZ.

  Peace, beldam! If there be
  One spark of natural feeling in thy breast,
  Forbear thy cruel words, but take thy child,
  And tend her with some charity.

PEPITA.

      Never again
  Shall she darken my tent!

She who preferr'd
The stranger to me,
His let her be!
Take her, and learn
The blessings that come
With a thing which is stolen.
My days are but few;
The tribe of my people
Shall know me no more.
For woe from the young
May be shaken away,
And happy old age
Be protracted for long
But sorrow on age
Swiftly doth ride
To the jaws of the grave;
As fruit which is ripe
Needs but to be shaken
To fall to the ground.

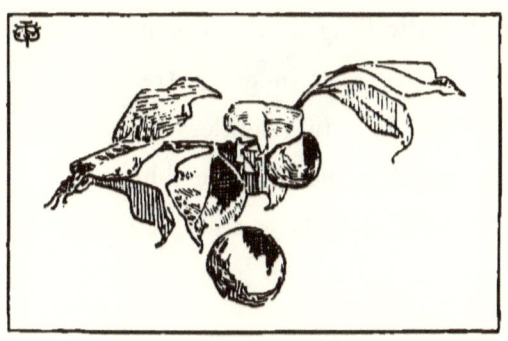

ACT II.

SCENE I.

Sunset. A vaulted room in a private house in Logroño. Books strewn about. Furnaces, alembics, crucibles, bellows, stills, stuffed reptiles and birds, and the furniture of an Alchemist's laboratory.

[Enter ALCALDE and PEDRO.]

PEDRO.

This is the dwelling of the wondrous man,
Whose help we seek in our extremity.
Here are his days in thankless toil consumed
O'er hot alembic and o'er crucible.
Here he seeks out the secrets of the earths,

The divers virtues of herbs, barks, and roots;
And here at night by constant lamp he pores
O'er musty books and crabbed manuscripts.

ALCALDE.

Strange that a man should leave the flowery fields,
The sweet companionship of fellow men,
Withering the marrow of his noonday life
O'er senseless books and glowing furnaces!
What is this man, I pray? and wherefore here
Has he his dwelling? Say, what is known of him?

PEDRO.

But little, sir. Some years ago he came
With all his property in many wains,
Chose out this house, as being fenced about
And hidden from the gazers of the street.
Since which he scarcely once has stirr'd abroad.
One single servant, very old, and mute
By nature or his master's orders, waits
His scanty wants, and gathers from the fields
The plants and stones to serve his master's ends.
The priest, good father John, one day, impell'd
By chance, or whim, or curiosity,
Entered the house, and being, as we, alone,
Turned to these books you see upon the shelves.
Some few he knew by sight, by hearsay more;
But most in languages unknown to him,

K

And letters quaint and singular, were writ.
The master enter'd sad and courteous.
Then, says the father, such a flood of lore
Roll'd from his lips, of foreign lands and books—
Not forced, but rising as the occasion rose—
As he had never heard nor dream'd before.
Since when the learned fathers often come
When they lack knowledge on some knotty point
Or need some rare book for their monast'ry;
He sells, though seeming to care naught for gold.

ALCALDE.

Perchance he makes it. I have some time heard
That, by long study, vigils, patience, toil,
It has been possible to gather in
Such wisdom in the ways of natural things
That at the last the great arcanum dawns
Upon the soul, and gold obeys the call.

[*Enter* ALVAREZ.]

ALVAREZ.

Good day, my masters! what are your behests?

ALCALDE.

First, learned sir, forgive our forwardness
Thus to intrude upon your privacy.
But I, first magistrate of this fair town—

Fair once, alas! but now how deeply fallen!—
Would fain be told by your own proper lips
What you do here.

ALVAREZ.

      No harm to man or thing.

ALCALDE.

Nay! but I ask it much for your own sake;
For idle rumour of the ignorant folk
Is busy with your doings. Since this plague
Has warped their judgment by calamity,
They even say that death doth lurk within
These silent walls—that noxious vapours rise
From these alembics. Even threats are heard
From the enfeebled creatures of the streets,
To burn your house and smite you unto death.
Therefore I ask, that I may speak to them
And hush the fury of their harass'd minds.

ALVAREZ.

I thank you deeply; yet I do not doubt
That idle tongues will soon find idle themes.
As for the plague you speak of, by my word
I even knew not that it was abroad;
Else surely had I striven by word and deed
To lend whatever little help I might.

ALCALDE.

> But, pardon me again! You tell me not
> Why you have so shut out the busy world.

ALVAREZ.

> Ask me not this, I pray you! aught but this.
> For there are motives in the hearts of all
> Which are not good to hear nor good to tell.
> May this suffice—my deeds do harm to none.
> If you can bring one charge against me, speak!
> And I will frankly stand on my defence.
> If not, I pray you let me be in peace
> To go my way, however tongues may wag.

ALCALDE.

> If you have reasons which you may not tell,
> I cannot press you further; yet perchance
> You will reply upon the other point,
> Which touches me as being a magistrate—
> Namely, the way in which you pass your time.

ALVAREZ.

> Freely and willingly I tell you this.
> In studying nature's laws and man's ideas.

ALCALDE.

> Seek you the stone of the philosopher?

ALVAREZ.

> I do.

ALCALDE [*to* PEDRO].

Ha! notest thou this, my friend?

PEDRO.

I note it well, and something else I note.

ALCALDE.

> Then can you, if I do not ask too much,
> Show me a fragment of this precious stone ?

ALVAREZ.

> See here. [*Points to his books.*]

ALCALDE.

> I see there merely books.

ALVAREZ.

> Books ! "merely books !" nothing but books ! My
>   friend,
> These are the stones of the philosophers ;
> For in the rolling tide of time and change
> These have endured, all else being swept away,
> Even as in river-beds the crumbling rocks
> Are ground to clay and sand and disappear,
> While the hard stones, though broken by the flood,
> Are smooth'd and polish'd. As they still endure,
> So live these books ; their lore is like the gem,
> To me a fable and uncoveted,
> Whose touch should turn the dullest dross to gold.

ALCALDE.

> I am rebuked ; but still I 've heard it said
> That those philosophers who most despise
> The stone we speak of, seek with ceaseless zeal

The subtle liquid which gives life and strength,
Renews our youth, and brings the glow of health,
Even when the article of death is heard.

ALVAREZ.

That I am seeking; that have I partly found.

ALCALDE.

Ha! now, indeed, you give encouragement.

ALVAREZ.

Seest yon alembic with the fire below ?
  Seest thou the charcoal slowly waste to ash ?
Seest thou its light? feel'st thou its sullen glow ?
  Mark'st thou the drops that grow, and fall, and
    splash ?
One drop of that upon your tongue would send
Your soul to seek another world, my friend.

ALCALDE.

I see it all. I 've seen it all before.

ALVAREZ.

Yet look again, and be thou very sure !
Know'st thou why that charcoal kindles ?
  Know'st thou whence its heat is got ?
Know'st thou why it glows and dwindles ?
  Know'st thou this, or know'st thou not ?

Know'st thou why the oil should rise
    Above the water? why, when tasted,
The spirit shrinks, the body dies,
    And all is rudely devastated?

ALCALDE.

    Well! charcoal burns, is hot and bright;
    That's the cause of heat and light.
    The oil is light; and so it floats,
    Like cork or bubbles, wood or boats.
    Some oils are poisonous; poisons kill;
    And when one dies the pulse is still.

ALVAREZ.

    My God, 'tis true! how little more know I
    Than thou who thus dost pass it glibly by.
    How little have we won from the dark fields
        Of the chaotic cosmos of the world!
    How scant the harvest that our sowing yields!
        How dense the curtain which still hangs unfurl'd!

ALCALDE.

    But that, my friend, is surely not the draught
    Which youth and strength doth bring to us when
        quaff'd?

ALVAREZ.

    Man! in the seeking after natural truth,
        In gaining wisdom, lies the germ of life.

His is a blooming and perennial youth —
  For him is Nature with renewal rife—
Who at her knees for ever humbly kneels,
Heark'ning the truth her loving heart reveals.
Seek, seek for knowledge! Ah! full well I know
Therein alone may lie the cure of woe.

ALCALDE.

It may be so. I understand you not;
But I am satisfied there is no harm
In your employments; and time presses me.
I also come, hearing of your repute,
To ask your aid in our most hapless strait.

ALVAREZ.

Speak, then, I pray you. If it be the plague
Which has attack'd the city, I may help;
For I am come from Egypt, where it broods
For ever like a vulture o'er the land.

ALCALDE.

It is, indeed. An awful pestilence
Has ravish'd half our homes; for full a month
Has it been waxing, knowing no abate.
The dead lie all unburied in the streets.
The shameless dogs prowl glutted with foul food.
The old, with trembling limbs, cast out their young,
To be in turn cast out by children's hands.

L

The mother shuns her infant if she thinks
There be a plague-taint in its poor young blood.
Children drive forth their parents from their doors;
While thieves, half crazed with terror and with
   wine,
Prowl unmolested through the public ways.
Horrible birds, unknown to us before,
Dispute with curs each blotch'd and rotting corpse.
Justice is paralysed, the time unhinged.
The decencies of life are cast aside.
Death, which is wont to come with sober thought,
And be wrapp'd up in reverence and awe,
Is hail'd with jesting and with ribaldry;
The chants and masses for departed souls
Are turned to lewdness and profanity.

ALVAREZ.

Horrible! strange and most unnatural.
Tell me, I pray you, when the ill first strikes,
How doth the malady declare itself?

ALCALDE.

In giddiness, a loathing for all food,
But thirst unquenchable, a fearful pain
Across the groins, a fouling tongue and breath;
Then doth the aching body 'gin to swell,
Turn crimson, bloated, dabbled with green spots;
And so come death and rotting in an hour.

ALVAREZ.

Great God of heaven! it is the very same!

ALCALDE.

Alas! he's struck; and we have brought with us
The foul contagion from the outer air.

ALVAREZ.

Yes, I am struck, but yet not as you think.
Tell me, is there a gypsy camp at hand?

ALCALDE.

Assuredly there is; why do you ask?
Would you seek aid among that thievish crew?
'Tis said, indeed, that some of them are skill'd
In philters and such shameless practices;
But for aught wholesome or medicinal
I doubt if thence much comfort may be drawn.

ALVAREZ.

Yet among them I go to find some means
To stay this plague. In five hours from this time
Meet me again. Now heaven be with you, sir!

ALCALDE.

Farewell! I shall assuage the burghers' wrath,
Who clamour for your death. But if, indeed,
You find for us some potent antidote
To stay our troubles, rich be your reward.

[ALCALDE *goes.*]

[PEDRO *approaches* ALVAREZ *and scans him closely.*]

PEDRO.

'Tis true! thou art the man.

Thou art my friend, my more than brother once.

Changed to old age in but a score of years—

Thy brow, once smooth and polish'd as a slab,

Now cross'd and furrow'd like a harrow'd field—

Thy step elastic and thy crest erect,

Now turned to weary paces and bent back—

Thou art the father of thy former self.

ALVAREZ.

I knew thee, Pedro, thou art little changed.

With thee the course of time has kindly dealt;

For days of peace, in wearing us away,

Leave us enfeebled, yet in else unchanged;

But care and sorrow eat into our hearts,

Corrode, distort, disfigure, and destroy.

PEDRO.

Tell me, my friend, what cares have weighed on
thee ?

For since thy flight naught has been heard of thee,

And silent rumour spoke of thee as dead.

ALVAREZ.

'Tis a long task, and all unprofitable.

Yet as thou hast my secret, and my life

Rests in thy hands, 'tis fittest I should speak ;
For a half confidence is more unsafe
Than total ignorance or total trust.
When twenty years ago I fled this town
(Fled as a murderer, though my hands were clean ;
For I could never hope to clear myself
Without accusing one more dear than life),
I dwelt among the gypsy tribe which then
Haunted the neighbourhood. As one of them
I lived and travell'd even as their chief and king ;
For I did wed the daughter of their king,
Who had been dead for many years before :
Her mother died, because she hated me,
Cursing her daughter for her love of me.
  One happy year, one year of supreme bliss
Was ours ; one son was born to us.
Alas ! I cannot, dare not, even think—
I scarcely know whence rose the coldness first :
Some quarrel, like a little distant cloud,

Which, growing fast, o'erspreads the firmament ;
Some small indignity much brooded o'er,
Yet in itself so small that it had pass'd

Like summer lightning, but amongst our tribe
Were busy, envious, and malicious tongues,
Who brook'd not that a stranger ruled o'er them.
Coldness begot contempt; contempt got hate.
Three cruel years I wander'd, strengthen'd still
By the sweet memory of my vanish'd love,
Until at last my secret enemies
Sought my destruction by the poison-cup.
I fled, and wander'd many weary years
From Spain still onward even to furthest Ind,
Arabia, Persia, and the Eastern lands—
Sometimes consorting with the gypsy tribes,
But ever drowning memory of my grief
In patient study of mankind and things.
Yet, though the body travell'd without rest,
My heart of hearts was left behind in Spain.
So, after years, am I return'd to drag
The remnant of my blighted life away
Here, 'midst these books and this obscurity.

PEDRO.

A piteous tale, indeed !
Hast thou not heard whether thy wife still lives,
If lives the child of this ill-sorted match ?

ALVAREZ.

No word of news have I.
But, as the Alcalde spoke, a horrid fear

Shot through my breast as baleful meteor-flash.
This pestilence which has laid bare the town
Accords most closely with diseases wrought
By gypsy poison; and the fearful thought
Will not be put aside, that my own tribe
By gypsy artifice has worked this ill.

PEDRO.

A frightful deed, if it in sooth be so.
Now I bethink me, gypsies have been seen
Prowling about the fountains of the street.
But they were not molested; it was thought
They came to plunder there the helpless dead,
Who lay about the wells in festering heaps,
Whither they crawl'd to slake their burning thirst.

ALVAREZ.

It must be so. This very hour I go
Straight to their camp. I shall conceal myself,
And gain their secret from their treacherous heart.
Meanwhile be cautious! Waste not idle fears,
But bid all men refrain from public wells,
Drinking alone what springs from private grounds.

PEDRO.

I go to bid the Alcalde see to this.

[PEDRO *goes.*]

ALVAREZ.

When, righteous Heaven! when shall my sorrow
  cease?
When shall my way of trouble know a wending?
Here, where I sought forgetfulness and peace,
  Is trouble's increase, but not trouble's ending.
May not the anguish of a score of years
  Be weigh'd against the hour of my trans-
    gression?
Cannot the waters of my silent tears,
  With self-upbraiding and contrite confession,
Wipe off the curse the dying mother spoke,
  The awful curse? Ah, no! it is fulfilling.
Heavier and deadlier weighs its doleful yoke,
  Nor shall my heart know rest before its stilling.
I feel that all in vain has been my strife,
  Vain as a bird's within the meshes striving.
I feel that now across my autumn's life
  The clouds of death are lowering fast and
    driving.

SCENE II.

About midnight. The same as Scene II., Act I.

[*Enter* ALVAREZ.]

ALVAREZ.

> Hast thou, O earth, among thy deepest caves,
> One most remote from all humanity,
> Where blackest night and desolation dwell—
> Where, through the long and slow revolving year.
> No hunter's footstep and no woodman's song
> Can penetrate, but where the ravenous wolf
> Hies him to munch his loathsome midnight meal
>
> There, with no comrade but my bitter woe,
> No hope in life but the swift end of life.

M

No fear of death but that it be not death,
Lull'd by the weeping from the marble rocks,
I 'd lay me down to cast this weary slough;
There, like an infant overwrought in grief,
I 'd sob, and sob, and sob myself to sleep.

Hither, a plaything of outrageous fate,
The time has toss'd me. Here, long years ago,
The consummation of my life was wrought;
And here, I feel it, shall dark death outstrip,—
Even as the body of a swimmer drown'd,
After long days of drifting to and fro,
Returns unto the spot from which he sprang.

These very trees were witness of my love;
They murmur in the moonlight as of yore.
But what of old seemed lullaby of love,
Breathes now in wailing cadence through the air.
So change the voices of inanimate things—
Changed by man's ceaseless mutability,
Until heart-echoes seem like nature's voice.

Here, by the secret tokens on the trees,
Must be the trysting-place to-night; and here
Must I secrete myself to overhear
Their gypsy councils. By this rock I 'll lurk.
Even now methinks I hear their voices near,
With their swift footsteps on the autumn leaves.

They come! they come! Now, heart, be still
awhile!

Enter GYPSIES *(armed, and with quenched*
torches), REA, *and* SALAZAR.

REA *soliloquizes.*

REA.

His love was subtlest ferment of my life,
Turning the sweetest honey of my youth
To strongest mead, which through my warm young
veins
In fervent joy career'd. My throbbing soul
Was girt about with glamorous clouds of love,
Through which the unreal world shone far and dim,
But, as the strongest, blandest mead, when sour'd,
Turns to the eagerest draught, so chang'd my love,
Neglected and despised, to deepest hate.
Yea, from the ashes of that love arose,
Even as the fabled Phœnix of the East
Rises from out the cinders of its sire,
Another passion. But how dire the change!
A vulture from the ashes of the dove,
A croaking raven from the throstle's nest.

Addresses the GYPSIES.

REA.

The time is ripe;
The seed we sowed

In blood and tears,
Bears now its fruit
Of blood and tears;
It but awaits
The sickle's edge.
You heard but now,
Our foes are low;
They lie like sheep
When murrain stalks
Among the folds.
Accursed race!
Not one shall live
To tell the tale;
For all shall fall.
But men shall ask
In after years
What mean the stones
Which they shall find,
The only trace
Of that which was.
The riven cup,
The chok'd-up well,
The crumbling gates,
The blacken'd walls,
Where thirsty flame
Has leapt and lick'd—
These shall proclaim
How gypsies hate.

Gird your loins!
And whet your knives!
For they shall drink
Their glut of blood.

To-morrow, ere
The break of day,
When they who tend
The sick, are sunk,

From weary watch,
To fever sleep,
Faint with grief
For what has fallen,
Faint with fear
For what may fall—
Then shall we break,
With brandish'd knives
And horrid cries,
Wild in their midst.
The night shall aid ;
And dreary fear
Will think it sees
Unchained fiends
Let loose from hell.

Spare not the babe
Which is coil'd in the arms
Of its mother asleep !

Spare not the bride,
Half-drunken in dreams
Of the morrow and bliss !

Spare not the old,
Though his breath may not last
Till the breaking of morn !

All, all shall fall !

Then fire shall devour
Their dwellings apace !

Draw your sharp knives !
Blunt be their edge
Ere you sheathe them again !

SALAZAR.

But, mother ! when the task is done,
When all the cursed race is fallen,
Swift vengeance shall our steps pursue ;
Nor savage glen, nor arid waste,
Shall shield us from the fell pursuit
Of justice and the peasants' spite.

REA.

When yet had gypsy justice ?
Is not the wolf of more esteem than we ?
Him troubles not the hunter in his lair,
But shuns him rather and his bony den.
The bear is met in open fight and slain,
Nor malice nor oppression in the strife ;
But we are driven like lepers from the fairs,
Are shunn'd and humbled in the market-place ;
And when we look upon a little child,
The mother snatches it, and, chiding, cries,
"Aroint thee, gypsy witch of evil eye."

SALAZAR.

Yet, mother, yet from this hour forth

A double hardship waits upon our path—
Not mere injustice and contempt,
But red revenge of cord and steel.

[REA, *aside.*]

Thou mongrel whelp of tigress and of ram,

[*aloud.*]

For this has been provided.
When our huge measure of revenge is full,
We leave this land of fair, false-hearted fools,
To cross the narrow sea. Morocco's king
Shall give our tribe a welcome and a home.
A people wild and free as we is there.
There shall we find a place of rest and peace.
On ! on ! my children; 'tis your queen who calls.

[GYPSIES *sing and gradually light their torches.*]

Chorus of GYPSIES.

See the red moon, sinking,
Hides her face from the earth !

On! for slaughter and drinking!
  On! for fury and mirth!

Think of your friends regretted!
  Think of your mother's tears!
Let each blade be whetted
  With the hate of a hundred years!

Strike! nor stint your slaying;
  But, in their faces white,
Dash your knives as they're praying,
  And smite again, and smite!

Spare them not for their weeping!
  Every tear they shed
Mix with a blood-drop, leaping
  Hot from the heart and red!

Spare them not for their lying!
  Sick and weak in the room!
Yell in the ears of the dying
  Tidings of bloody doom.

Tear the maid from the altar!
  Tear the babe from the teat!
A curse on him who shall falter
  To trample it under his feet!

See the red moon, sinking,
   Hides her face from the earth !
On ! for slaughter and drinking !
   On ! for fury and mirth !

[REA, SALAZAR, *and* GYPSIES *hurry off.*]

SCENE III.

Midnight. Same as Scene I., Act I.

Enter Pedro *and* Alcalde *conversing.*

Alcalde.

All has been done which lies within my power:
At all the public wells a guard is placed.
Of the few trusty burghers that can stir.

Pedro.

I saw them as I passed: a hard task theirs;
Themselves but scarce recover'd from the plague,
Fever'd and feeble, to hold back the throng

Of the mad creatures clamorous for drink,
Who threaten, yea, and with their feeble hands
Would tear the guardians of the wells away.

ALCALDE.

Poor, frenzied wretches! other men are placed
At all the chiefest crossings. In their hands
They carry buckets from my private well,
And give to all who thirst.

PEDRO.

                    Have you not heard
If Alvarez be come? methinks 'tis time :
I grow uneasy at his lengthen'd stay.

ALCALDE.

'Twere well for him if he did not return,
At least until the plague has left the land;
For when I told the people what you said
Alvarez had directed, they were wild,
Believed it not, but said it was a snare
To kill them cruelly with burning thirst.

                    [*Enter* ALVAREZ *hurriedly.*]

ALCALDE.

Well met at last!

ALVAREZ.

To arms! away, to arms!
Summon the citizens from every house,
But yet with silence.
Bid all the people come—
All who can wield a sword or hold a knife,
Let them all gather hither where we stand.

ALCALDE.

But why, my friend? against this pestilence
Steel has no power.

ALVAREZ.

To arms! I say, to arms!
The gypsies follow closely on my heels—
Five hundred strong—
To plunder, slay, and burn.
I come in hot haste from their midnight camp.
Ask me no more! to arms! to arms! to arms!

ALCALDE.

Five hundred! say you so?
Stay, let me think awhile!

ALVAREZ.

Think not, but act!

ALCALDE.

"He who acts surely
First thinks maturely."

Ha, so! I have it.

Go all and bid each man you meet

Summon his neighbour; bid him summon his:

Bid all repair with arms, it boots not what,

To this same spot, this very market-place.

Divide them, Pedro, into equal bands,

Even as they come, and place a band in three

Of the four streets which run together here.

I go to close all gates but the one way

Whence leads the Seville road; this the most

    straight

And longest way about. Now haste away.

                [*Exeunt* ALCALDE *and* PEDRO.]

        Enter BURGHERS *armed.*

ALVAREZ.

And I, what task is mine?

Nay, I must shake the horror from my heart,

And do my utmost for the common weal.

    [*The* BURGHERS *whisper together, and point to*
            ALVAREZ. ALVAREZ *will go.*]

1st BURGHER.

Stay, wretched man!

2nd BURGHER.

Stay, cursed wizard!

3rd BURGHER.

    Stay, murderer!

1st BURGHER.

    Art thou not he
    Who broodest ever over dusty toils
    Shunning the daylight and the face of men?

ALVAREZ.

    I am. What then?

2nd BURGHER.

Art thou not he
Who canst distil from harmless plants and flowers
Poisons most subtle to corrupt the blood ?

ALVAREZ.

I am. What then ?

2nd BURGHER.

What then ? Why, then
Thou art the cause of all our misery.
Thou hast given rise to this most fatal plague
By drugs and pharmacies. Thou hast charged the
    air
With deadliest vapours and corrupting fumes.

ALVAREZ.

'Tis false! you lie!

1st BURGHER.

Thou art the man who bade our simple Mayor
Close all the public fountains of the streets,
That we might die of thirst. Thou art the man.

3rd BURGHER.

Let me look closer, friends! Why, what is this ?
Thou art the man, or else my memory fails,
Who, twenty years ago, did slay our Count,
And fledst the city.

ALVAREZ.

I am the man you think;
But yet I did——

3rd BURGHER.

But now shalt thou be hang'd!

ALVAREZ.

O, cruel fools! what curse so dire and black
Can fall on man as the one curse of folly?

3rd BURGHER.

The curse of wickedness! down on your knees and
    pray.
What! fearing punishment for thy misdeed
Thou fledst the city. Dost thou in monstrous
    spite,
After these many years have pass'd us by,
Now turn on us, and blight this once fair town,
Conspire on plague to heap contagion
By thy most damn'd devices? Bear him forth!

[*Enter* ALCALDE *and* PEDRO.]

ALCALDE.

Now all is well prepared! Ha, what is this?

[*Perceives dispute.*]

ALVAREZ.

> Out, blind infatuation! are your minds
> More foully fester'd than your bodies are.
> Listen! My God! they come!

ALCALDE.

> I shall inquire another time in this. [*All listen.*]
> 'Tis true, they come; from the last gate I saw
> Their torches gleam, and heard their naked feet
> Upon the hard pav'd road. See ye yon light?
> Disperse yourselves; away to ambuscade!
> Then, when they reach this central market-place,
> Fall on them suddenly with sword and knife.
>
> > [*All hide.*]

Enter GYPSIES *(tumultuously with torches and armed),*
REA, *and* SALAZAR.

REA.

> > See ye yon house?
> > There dwelleth he
> > Who bitterly wrong'd
> > My people and me.
> > Burn it, and smite
> > All who essay
> > To rush from the doors.
> > Let not one soul
> > See the sun dawn.

[*Armed* BURGHERS, *with* ALCALDE, ALVAREZ, *and* PEDRO, *rush on.*]

ALVAREZ.

Ha! treason! treason!

[BURGHERS *and* GYPSIES *fight.* ALVAREZ *is wounded.* ALVAREZ *and* PEDRO *are surrounded by* GYPSIES, *who are then driven off.*]

.

SCENE IV.

Dawn.   Same place as SCENE II., ACT II.

Enter GYPSIES *carrying* ALVAREZ *wounded and leading*
PEDRO *bound.* SALAZAR *dead.* REA.

REA.

> Lay him beneath
> The spreading chestnut-branches.
> There let the wretch
> Gasp out his traitor-soul.
> Vengeance, though late,
> At last has overtaken
> Him who despised
> My people and my crown.

Vengeance, alas!
For ye for whom 'twas summon'd,
Sightless are ye
And dumb in sudden death.
Blacken'd and gash'd
In yonder cursed city,
Shall ye not hear
The tidings of revenge?
Shall ye not wake
To see him who betray'd ye
Prostrate in shame
And mortal agony?
This is the hour
Foretasted in long waiting;
Grav'd on the stars
By hand of destiny.
This is the hour
Whose coming, like a beacon,
Shone through long years
Of anguish and despair.
Speak, then, my soul!
Wherefore dost thou tremble
Like a base hound
Beneath a thunder-storm?

PEDRO.

See! his pale lips
Are tremblingly parted, and echo

Faintly the things which float through his
　　suffering soul,
　　As the dim thoughts
　Fade and revive like a taper,
Flickering awhile ere it sinks in the dead of the
　　night.

ALVAREZ.

　　Like the streamlet at our feet
　　　Our love shall be ;
　　Every hinderance it meet
　　　Shall wake new harmony.

　　Every rapid, every lake
　　　Shall be fairer than the last ;
　　Yet so like that it shall wake
　　　Thought of the past.

REA.

Memory of unutterable wrong !
Scorn and desertion ! weary wandering life !
Each gibe that ever on my people's name
Was heap'd, each injury be with me now !
　　　　Lest my heart break !

Plunge every feeling traitor to my wrath
Into the glowing furnace of my wrong,
That the rebellious throbbings of remorse
Be hush'd in hate's inexorable fire,
　　　　Lest my heart break !

Peace! ah! be still; it is too late!
Away regret! the deed is done!
Blood on my hands! blood on my head'
Blood on my soul! a husband's blood!

PEDRO.

Listen! again
Are sounding, more distant and faintly,
The chords of his bosom, like strings of the harp
of the winds,
When the high storm
Wrings from them, sobbing and breaking,
Music more wild, yet as sweet as the zephyr
awoke.

ALVAREZ.

Like the evening o'er our heads
Our love shall be;
Where each glittering planet spreads
Its rays in majesty.

Every day shall greet our eyes
With new delight,
As every hour fresh stars arise
To deck the night.

REA.

O! thou hast never in thy worst abuse,
By coldness or more palpable contempt,

Plunged such a poison'd dagger in my breast,
Nor scar'd my soul with such hot agony
                As with these words—

Which echo too distinctly in my heart,
Dragging in anguish long-forgotten thoughts—
Forgotten or long choked with weeds of hate,
Or overrun by nightshade of revenge.—
                To glaring day.

Lie hidden, memory of vanish'd love!
Was I the first to break the vows we made?
Did I first wander from the sunny paths?
Were the bright flowers of rapture and content
                First crush'd by me?

O! if my heart be guilty as thine own,
If at my hands not only death but wrong
Were wrought upon thy no more guilty head,
Thy death were murder, and my life were woe—
                Woe without end!

PEDRO.

                Late! all too late!
        The building has sunk in its glory,
        Devour'd by the swift-leaping flames of thy
                hatred and rage.
                Sprinkle no more
        The water of ruth on the ashes.

The halls and the columns shall never be lifted
again.

ALVAREZ.

Like the bindweed and the sun
Our love shall be;

When his course of light is run,
Her soul shall flee.

P

When the faithful constant flower
Hangs her fair head,
He knows no life beyond that hour—
His course is sped.

REA.

By thy side behold me kneeling,
By thy side thy weeping wife !
Spare him, death ! O ! spare my husband !
For each drop of blood thou sparest
Take a thousand drops of mine.
Speak ! O speak ! say that thou livest !
Bid me breathe, and bid me hope
That by long and deep devotion,
That by humbleness and meekness,
I may win thy love again.

The lips that speak are crimson gashes ;
All their words are drops of blood,
Every drop proclaiming murder.
Is this, then, the only answer
Which the husband gives the wife ?
God of heaven ! I have denied Thee,
Scorn'd Thy handiwork and word.
Now I know that Thou existest ;
For my prayers were empty, fruitless,
Did they not ascend to Thee.

ALVAREZ.

> Like the swallow and the fall——
> Ah, me! ah, me! ah, me!   [*Dies.*

PEDRO.

> 'Tis past! The hour
> Of vengeance, too ruthless and bloody,
> Is written in murder and guile; but his wrong-
>   bearing soul,
> Like a struck deer,
> All bleeding and panting and fleeing,
> Plunges for rest in the river's more merciful
>   tide.
>   [*Pause.*]

PEDRO [*to* REA].

> 'Tis done! but not yet.
> No; not for weary centuries of years
> Shall the deep curse which rests upon thy race,
> Now trebly doubled by thy deed of wrath,
> Be wiped away. Thy name shall be borne down
> The course of time drench'd with the hard-wrung
>   tears
> Of thine own people; and the contemptuous hate
> Of all the nations shall pursue thy race,
> Hearthless and houseless.
> Should ever pity at their sad estate
> Be born to men, thy manes shall arise,

And, as a horrid spectre murder-brow'd,
Shall sear their hearts with hate's unfading fire.

                              [*Pauses.*]
                  [*Noise of* BURGHERS *approaching.*]
                           [*The* GYPSIES *escape.*]

PEDRO.

    Even now!
    Hark! from the city
    The burghers are pouring to rescue—
    To rescue too late, but yet not too late for revenge.
    Woman, thou diest!

REA.

                " Diest!"
    There is a mark upon the shore of life
    Which, being flooded by the tide of grief,
    Points to the hour of death.
    Beyond that hour no heart may dare to beat,
    But, turning backward, must seek out again
    The home from which it came.

            Silence and night,
            Unfold your shadowy wings!
            Rest, sleep, night, nought,
            Is all the heaven I ask.
            Or if, indeed, there be
            Another life in death,

Spirit of him who once
Was more than life to me,
Grant me this prayer alone:
Beest thou in heaven,
Then at the gates of heaven
Let me for ever weep!
If in the heart of hell,
Then in the heart of hell
Let me for ever weep!

[*Stabs herself and falls.*]

PEDRO.

On the earth, in the deep,
In the round of the heavens,
There is naught which brings forth
Of its kind so abundantly
As blood spilt unrighteously.

Be it hid in the caves
Seldom trod in the forests,
Be it scatter'd at night
On the waves that roll stormily
O'er the sea that is fathomless—

Be it drunk by the blasts
Blowing dry from the deserts,
Or burn'd by the fire
When men standing fearfully
Behold their homes smouldering—

The seed which is sown,
Though tardy its germing,
Some day shall arise
And bear fruit unfailingly,
Bloody and manifold.

[*As the sound of the approaching* BURGHERS *increases*
REA *raises herself.*]

REA.

I see it! Lo I see it coming, mighty!
As I have seen it in my childhood's dreams.
It is the same! the wave! the wave!

Flooding the face of ocean, endless, dark,
High as the heavens and fathomless as hell.
Upon its crest the wrecks of armaments
With ancient mountains wrested from their roots,
Midst spires and lofty domes, the pride of men,
Are toss'd like bubbles. From out its foamy sides
Uncouth sea-monsters glare upon the day,

Startled unwilling from their weedy lairs
Where, ages long, unknown to man, they lurk'd
Hostile to light. Now onward with a groan,
That shakes the tottering earthball to its core,
It soars. The ground recedes and sinks
To meet it. Death! death! I come! I come!

                                        [*Dies.*]

Marcus Ward & Co., Royal Ulster Works, Belfast.